I Really Want a Puppy Mum!

Melita Lovett-Sisson

Limited Special Edition. No. 6 of 25 Paperbacks

This is Melita Lovett-Sisson's first published book. A writer for the past 14 years, she has written many stories only told to family and friends. This is the first in the series of stories featuring Kev, a playful, naughty and mischievous little dog. Melita lives on the Central Coast in Australia with her husband and two children and has just realised her dream of being able to tell stories to children across the world.

I Really Want a Puppy Mum!

Melita Lovett-Sisson

AUSTIN MACAULEY PUBLISHERS™

LONDON • CAMBRIDGE • NEW YORK • SHARJAH

A CIP catalogue record for this title is available from the British Library.

ISBN 9781528933841 (Paperback)
ISBN 9781528933858 (Hardback)
ISBN 9781528967631 (ePub e-book)

www.austinmacauley.com

First Published (2019)
Austin Macauley Publishers Ltd
25 Canada Square
Canary Wharf
London
E14 5LQ

For my children, Tiarna and Jaden, my inspiration.

I really want a puppy Mum

I want one really bad.

Please say I can have a puppy Mum

Or I will be so sad.

I know that I have asked before
And each time you have said no.
I'm sure you'll change your mind this time
If you just give me a go!

I promise I can do it Mum

I'll do it all ! You'll see !

You won't have to do a thing

I'll take care of my puppy.

I promise I will feed it

14

And brush its coat each day.

16

I promise I will shut the gate

So it can't run away.

18

It doesn't have to be a big dog
Just a puppy, cute and small.

I'll teach it tricks, like beg and sit

22

And how to catch a ball.

24

I'll take my dog on walks each day

26

And clean up all its mess.

28

PLEASE can I have a puppy Mum?

30

Hooray, my mum said yes !

The End

34